For Shosh,

Warmly!

Alan

12/25/00

A BREEZE
IN THE WILLOWS

A BREEZE
IN THE WILLOWS

A celebration of the wit and wisdom
of *The Wind in the Willows*

Allen Johnson, Jr.
Illustrated by Roger Michell

TEN SPEED PRESS
Berkeley, California

TEN SPEED PRESS
P.O. Box 7123
Berkeley, CA 94707

Distributed in Australia by E.J. Dwyer Pty Ltd;
in Canada by Publishers Group West; in New Zealand by Tandem Press;
in South Africa by Real Books; and in the United Kingdom and Europe by Airlift Books.

Text and cover design by Nancy Austin
Printed in Hong Kong

Library of Congress Cataloging in Publication Data on file with publisher.

1 2 3 4 5—01 00 99 98 97

To Jill, with love.

–A. J.

For Chloe, Alice, and Charlie, with love.

–R. M.

CONTENTS

PREFACE

It is the human predicament that we are often unable to preserve what's best from the past. Thus, many good and beautiful things disappear in the relentless sweep of "progress." Occasionally, however, some work of man is so good and so beautiful that it must be preserved. Such a work is Kenneth Grahame's classic *The Wind in the Willows.*

I was introduced to *The Wind in the Willows* by my mother, who read it aloud to me during a childhood illness. It's not an easy book to read to a young child. The vocabulary is difficult; but somehow young and old alike are captivated by the beauty and warmth of the tale. What is it about this book that enables it to exert its charm and work its magic on children and adults?

The Wind in the Willows is about those aspects of life that we value most deeply. It's about the warmth of home and friendship and the beauty of nature. It's about the mystery of life. It's about the lure of adventure. It's about loving, helping, accepting, and forgiving. Oddly enough, it's about animals who are more "human," in the best sense of the word, than we humans often are. It is so well-written, with such poetic imagery, that it can be used as a guide to good writing.

More than this, it is an inspiring guide to life. It's wise, exciting, warm, fun, and, best of all, funny. Above all, Kenneth Grahame tells a wonderful story, making the characters so real to us that we feel we know them. We come to care deeply about Mole, Toad, Ratty, and Badger. These are just *some* aspects of the magic and mystery of *The Wind in the Willows.*

All of my life I have been entranced by a book that is supposed to be for children. I must confess this has made me wonder about myself at times—I suspect that it has to do with my never having completely grown up. In any event, I had long dreamed of doing *something* in association with this wonderful book. Since I hadn't a clue what it might be, however, I put this dream away and moved on to other things.

Years later, I was looking at the Ernest Shepard illustration of Mole and Ratty idling in a boat and was inspired to write a short verse, which I called "Perfect Summer Dream." I thought it was pretty good and that it went well with the illustration. Soon, I began to reexamine both the Shepard illustrations and Grahame's wonderfully poetic text as inspiration for other verses. Thus was born the idea of a book of verses as a companion piece to *The Wind in the*

Willows. I would try to be completely true to *The Wind in the Willows* and capture some of the essence of this great book in verse. "What should I call it?" I asked my wife. *"A Breeze in the Willows,"* she said at once.

When I was writing these verses, there was the question of how much of Grahame's language to use. I didn't worry too much over this question. Since my purpose was to capture some of the essence of the characters and the story in verse, I used the language that was most true to *The Wind in the Willows.* Some of the verses contain none of Grahame's language; some are a mixture of his language and mine; some—the most beautiful—are almost pure Grahame. I began a search for an illustrator.

It is sometimes the case that what you seek is right under your nose. Such was the case in finding the illustrator for *A Breeze in the Willows.* My wife, Jill, and I have a small cottage in Cornwall, England. One of our neighbors, Roger Michell, is an internationally known potter and artist whose work we greatly admire. Jill suggested I give a copy of the manuscript to Roger to see if he might be interested in doing the illustrations. Luckily, Roger, who has developed a decorative, "illustrative" style of pottery, had been wanting for some time to take his style "off of the pottery and onto the page." He sent us some preliminary pen-and-ink drawings of Mole, Ratty, Toad, and Badger, and they were wonderful. Roger had exactly the right feel for the characters and the setting. In addition to this, having him as a neighbor was an ideal situation for our collaboration. Things were falling into place.

Would Kenneth Grahame have approved of *A Breeze in the Willows?* He died in 1932, so I can't ask for his approval, but I believe I would have gotten it. I know he did enjoy another companion piece—a play by A. A. Milne called *Toad of Toad Hall,* which ran for many Christmas seasons in London. Milne reported that Kenneth Grahame and his wife watched the play and took great delight at hearing lines from the book come to life on the stage. While I am no A. A. Milne, I feel that I am in very good company when I follow a precedent set by him. I know that these verses have been written and illustrated with great love and respect for Mole, Rat, Badger, and Toad, and for Grahame's story, and I feel that we have been true to the original book. I hope that in celebrating the wit and wisdom of *The Wind in the Willows,* these verses and Roger Michell's illustrations will inspire many to read or reread Grahame's wonderful work.

—Allen Johnson, Jr.

A BREEZE
IN THE WILLOWS

BOTHER AND O BLOW!

When a Mole must do spring cleaning,
He will work quite hard and so,
Moley shocked himself by saying:
"Bother and O blow!"

But his heart was filled with longing,
And his molish will was rent
By the soft insistent calling
Of spring's sweet discontent.

So the Mole said: "Hang spring cleaning!"
And he bolted from his home,
And he scratched and scrooged and scrabbled
Up through the fragrant loam.

And his snout popped into sunlight,
And thus it came to pass
That a Mole did roll in pure delight
In the warm, sweet meadow grass.

ONION SAUCE!

To show a bossy rabbit
That he is not the boss,
Give him Moley's insult—
Tell him: "Onion sauce!"

To quash a rabbit's repartee
And leave him at a loss,
Bowl him over, hurry on,
Jeering "Onion sauce!"

RATTY'S PLACE

Bijou dwelling set into the riverbank,
Roofed and sheltered by the emerald turf...

Beneath the door,
The friendly river gliding by.
Just inside
The twinkling of a tiny eye...

"Hullo Mole!" said Rat.

PERFECT SUMMER DREAM

A summer day…

The river slumbers,

Lulled by the sunny drone and hum of life.

A Mole, a Water Rat

Idle in a boat.

Mole, the sunlight baking on his fur,

Gazes deep into the lushness

Of the riverbank.

Ratty pauses on his oars to watch

A cool green circle swirl away…

A dragonfly stops time.

Eternal moment.

Perfect summer dream.

MOLE OVERBOARD

O squashy, pulpy, sodden, dismal Mole!
How quickly Ratty brings you to the shore,
How kindly, then, he dries you off,
How lightly he forgives what you have done,
How clearly you perceive his noble heart.

Thus is friendship born.

FIRESIDE CHAT

We think our cheerful fire has banished night,
And yet we really bask in friendship's light.

TOAD HALL

Handsome hall of softly mellowed bricks,
Soaring roofs and chimneys, parapets,
Noble, leaded windows,
Well-kept lawns
Reaching to the water's edge…

A suitable abode
For a highly singular Toad.

TOAD

Egotist,
Adventurer,
Menace on the road,
Dilettante
And hedonist—
The one and only Toad.

Passionate,
Incompetent,
To friends a heavy load…
Brash and brave,
Magnificent!
Incorrigible Toad.

THE VISION

A Toad converted! How? You well may ask us.
Can a Toad have his road to Damascus?

'Twas on a road his vision did appear,
A simple motorcar, and yet, oh dear,
It filled poor Toad with awe and love and lust.
"Poop poop!" it spoke
And vanished in the dust.

And Toad, transformed, gave answer by and by.
"Poop poop!" he breathed. "O bliss!
O my! O my!"

THE WILD WOOD

Looming, glooming shadow shapes—
Darkness creeps around him,
Pattering, whistling…
Ghostly noises hound him.

Lurking, smirking, hating, waiting
In their secret places,
Leering, peering from their holes,
Evil little faces.

And deep within the Wild Wood,
Lost beyond all doubt,
Mole hears the desperate warning:
"Get out, you fool, get out!"

BADGER'S KITCHEN

Well-festooned with hams
And bundled herbs
And nets of onions,
Dark above with blackened beams,
Yet glowing as the firelight burnished
Ruddy bricks
And copper pans
And polished wood…
Badger's kitchen held the friends.

Replete, they stretched before the fire
And lost themselves in talk.

TWO LITTLE HEDGEHOGS

Two little hedgehogs
Lost in the snow.
One's called Billy.
The other?
Don't know!

NOBLE BADGER

Noble Badger, strong and kind,
Protector of the small…
But noble deeds must wait—
He's winter's thrall,
And has to disappear.
Where is he?
In his study—
Being "busy"!

LOST CITY

Deep beneath the Wild Wood
The ancient city slept.
Columns, chambers, passages,
Silted over by the streams and freshets
From a thousand years of rains.
Layered down and down and down
By a thousand years of falling leaves.

"People lived here once,"
The Badger said.
"Here they walked and talked and slept,
Stabled horses,
Ventured forth to fight and trade…
A rich and powerful folk,
Builders who believed their city
Would be here forever."

"But what has become of them all?"
Asked the Mole.

HEED THE CALL
OF HOME

When the world is cold and lonely,
And we've lost our weary way, we must
Heed, heed, heed the call of home.

When a friend we love is calling,
Then we surely must obey. We must
Heed, heed, heed the call of home.

For home is like a loyal friend
Who patiently will wait
While off we go to find our destiny.
Yet home can be forgotten
While we circumnavigate
The earth in search of places to be free.

But life *does* come full circle,
And we find ourselves some day, when we
Heed, heed, heed the call of home.

BACKSLIDING TOAD

To cure a Toad of his obsession,
Badger him, extract confession,
Beg and reason, rave and rant—
No matter, he will just recant.

MALINGERER

A dying Toad this pitiful
Will never linger on.
Before you fetch the doctor,
He will certainly be gone!

DANGER!
OVERINFLATED TOAD

Conceited? Yes,

He's so puffed up

One fears he may explode!

An ever-present danger

When a toad's too full of Toad.

ALAS, A TOAD
HAS COME TO GRIEF!

How high inflated toads can float.
How far they have to fall,
And Toad, the terror of the road,
Fell farthest of them all.

By commandeering motorcars,
Poor Toady came to grief,
Caught and judged and sentenced
As a lowly, common thief,

And put in jail for twenty years
To languish and to weep
In the deepest, darkest dungeon,
In the best-guarded keep
In all the length and breadth of Merry England.

O, THE BLESSED COOLNESS!

Midsummer night with cooling fingers
Brushed away the lingering pools of sullen heat.
Moley, resting on the riverbank,
Panting from the torrid afternoon,
Felt their soothing touch.
Soon his friend arrived and sat with him
And gazed across the blackness
Of the river's satin swirls.
"O, the blessed coolness!" Ratty said.

PIPER AT THE
GATES OF DAWN

The two small creatures
Looked upon the Helper.
Dazed by love and awe,
They crouched before Him
Worshipping.
Then they were dazed again
By golden sunlight
Flooding through the marsh.
When sight returned,
The vision was no more.
Lest they be overwhelmed by loss,
A soft capricious breeze
Touched them with a final gentle gift:
Forgetfulness.

TEA AND TOAST

A Toad who's sunk in bleak despair
Must certainly be dosed
With steaming cups of fragrant tea
And stacks of buttered toast.

The jailer's daughter knew her Toad
And brought him tea and toast,
And Toad, his spirits quite restored,
Became the genial host.

He told her of his stately home
'Til praise turned into boast,
And all from sipping fragrant tea
And munching buttered toast.

WHEN IS A TOAD
NOT A TOAD?

A Toad in washerwoman's dress
Looks better than you'd ever guess.
It does seem odd, but nonetheless,
Toad really looked quite charming.

The dress was flattering because
It covered certain toadish flaws,
And yet it gave poor Toady pause—
The likeness was alarming.

INCOGNITO

Decorum lost, and dignity,
And oh how it did rankle,
But still, a fleeing Toad must sometimes
Show a bit of ankle!

ADVICE

Be yourself, don't try to be another.
Remember that pretensions all are bosh.
A Toad who claims to be a washerwoman
May, in fact, be called upon to wash!

SWEET REVENGE

The woman on the barge was rude,
And pure contempt she showed,
With disrespectful epithets like
"Nasty, crawly Toad."

She grabbed poor Toady fore and aft,
And lo, a Toad took flight.
An airborne washerwoman-toad—
It must have been a sight.

But after Toady swam ashore,
Guile triumphed over force.
Toad had his solid sweet revenge—
He stole the woman's horse!

COME SOUTH WITH ME

Soon winter will be here,
Shivering sunless days of damp, chill air.

Come South with me!
To violet seas and tawny sands
And lizard-haunted walls.
Where villas glitter white
Against the olive woods,
Where emerald isles of wine and spice
Are set like jewels,
Low in languorous seas.

Come South with me, and we will swim
In sun-soaked airs of amber, rose, and aqua blue,
And feast and sing in balmy nights
Beneath great stars
In deep, black velvet skies.

THE BATTLE OF
TOAD HALL

"Follow me!" shouted Badger,
And they charged into the hall.
The revelers were taken by surprise.
"A Mole!" shouted Moley,
And Toad began to Whoop
His marrow-chilling, awful battle cries.

Desperate and determined,
Ratty joined in the fray.
In panic all the stoats and weasels fled.
The heroes swung their cudgels.
With fury they attacked,
And whacked at every stoat and weasel head.

Ferrets fled into the fireplace,
Weasels scrabbled up the wall,
There was squeaking, there was screeching,
At the battle of Toad Hall.

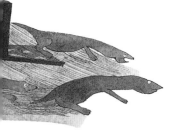

TOAD SONG

The song was sung in solitude,
But true to form, alas,
Gross exaggeration,
Self-praise, conceit, and gas—
A final ventilation
Of Toad the pompous ass—
The Ego's final, brightly burning flame.

His friends arrived and found a Toad
Of pure humility—
Albeit somewhat overdone…
"O noble, humble me!"
He was revered by one and all
The way a Toad should be.
The more we change, the more we stay the same.

GOOD NIGHT OLD FRIEND

Old friends must be revisited.
In books they're always home.
So don't forget these good old friends
No matter where you roam.

Old friends must be revisited,
But 'til we do, that's that.
"Good night old friend," said Moley.
"Good night old friend," said Rat.

— THE END —

ACKNOWLEDGMENTS

Thanks to John Mella, Mary Veazey, Chuck Ghigna,
Bobby Frese, Sally Hertz, George Young, my editor Clancy Drake, and
my wife Jill for their generous help and encouragement.